EDIRIN

Akpojotor Peter

Published in Nigeria
By
Pi Africana Press
pi.africanapress@yahoo.com
+23480 6894 4034

ISBN: 978-978-997-081-0

You can contact the author via:
07031870062, 08077118876
akpojotor.peter@gmail.com

DEDICATION

This play is dedicated to
all those who still uphold
the virtue of patience

CHARACTERS

Edirin	A young man.
Oke	Edirin's closest childhood friend.
Mrs. Titi	Edirin's mother.
Tejiri	Edirin's younger sister.
Mr. Akpi	Edirin's father.
Mrs. Elohor	Edirin's stepmother.
Miss Linda	Secondary school mathematics teacher.
Rume	Edirin's Secondary school classmate.
Andy **Ogaga** **Kome**	Internet fraudsters (yahoo boys)
King Koko	The traditional ruler of Uloho kingdom.
Chief Tovie **Chief Osiobe** **Chief Ofure**	Members of council of chiefs of Uloho Kingdom.
Igbogbo	A one-eyed juju priest.

SCENE ONE

Mrs. Titi's Compound

Mrs. Titi, is seated on a short stool in the veranda, extracting palm fruit concentrate which she wants to use in preparing banga *soup. Tejiri, her twelve-year-old daughter, is seated on the floor at the left corner of the veranda doing her school assignments; she finds one of the questions difficult to answer and takes it to her mother for help.*

Tejiri: Mummy, which is the auxiliary and which is the main verb in this sentence? *(Points to the sentence; holding the book close to her mother's face)*

Mrs. Titi: Will you take this book away from my face? You had the whole of the weekend to do your assignments and possibly get help on the ones you find difficult, you didn't do them, rather you played all through.

It's this evening that I'm busy, with oil all over my hands, that you are bringing your book to seek help for your assignment.

Tejiri: My teachers gave me lots of assignments. I did some yesterday *(Murmurs as she walks angrily back to where she was sitting and begins whimpering).*

Mrs. Titi: You should have brought it to me all this time that I was less busy, or don't you know that oil could have stained your book? And your classmates would laugh at you. *(Trying to pacify Tejiri)* Okay, read the question, let me see if I can help you.

Tejiri: My teacher said I should identify the auxiliary and the main verbs in these sentences numbered one to ten. I have done all except number eight.

Mrs. Titi: I know verbs are the action words in any sentence. *(Pauses for few seconds as she tries to recall what auxiliary verbs are; shakes her head)* I can't quite remember what auxiliary verbs are, but just read, let me see if I can do it for you. If I can't, you will keep it, when Edirin comes from where he went, he will do it for you.

Tejiri: The sentence is 'where were you going when I saw you last night?'

Mrs. Titi: 'Going' is a verb. 'Saw' is also a verb, but I don't know which is the main or auxiliary verb. When Edirin returns, show it to him and let him do it for you.

Tejiri: Okay, mum.

Mrs. Titi: Please, get me some water from the kitchen.

(Tejiri goes into the kitchen and returns with a cup of water)

Mrs. Titi: This water will not be enough. Pour it into that pot (*Points to the empty pot beside her*) and go get some more. This time, use that big red bowl.

(Edirin walks in from the entrance of the compound glowing with joy and approaches Mrs. Titi)

(Tejiri empties the cup of water into the pot and goes to get more as requested by her mother)

Edirin: Mum, I have been offered admission. They gave me my first choice, petroleum engineering.

Mrs. Titi: Wow! That is great! So, very soon, my son will become an engineer and I will be mama engineer.

Tejiri: (*As she returns with the bowl of water*) Mum, you will also be mama lawyer when I become a lawyer.

Mrs. Titi: Yes *o*, my daughter. I can't wait to become mama engineer and mama lawyer *o*. Meanwhile, before the day gets too dark, go and bring that your assignment so that Edirin will do it for you.

Tejiri: Okay, mum. *(Drops the bowl on the floor, close to her mother, and goes to get her books)*

Mrs. Titi: Edirin, first thing tomorrow, you will go and inform your father of your admission.

Edirin: What am I informing him for?

Mrs. Titi: He is your father. You have to tell him, so that he can raise money for your fees and accommodation for you.

Edirin: All the previous times that I have gone to meet him for money, he always says he doesn't have money.

Mrs. Titi: And do you know if he has money now?

Edirin: It's not as if he didn't have money those times that I went to him; he just didn't want to give me. For instance, he told me he didn't have money when I went to ask for money for my JAMB registration, only to buy a car two days later. *(Suddenly angry at the recollection of the incident)* Mum, I have made up my mind never to meet him for anything again.

Mrs. Titi: Meaning you don't want to go to the university. Because, I alone cannot raise money for your school fees, accommodation and feeding. Now, go and help your sister with her assignment. First thing tomorrow, you will go and inform your father of your admission. *(Rises from the stool she is sitting on, lifts the pot containing the palm fruit concentrate and walks towards the kitchen)*

(Edirin goes to Tejiri and begins to help her with her assignment)

Light fades.

SCENE TWO

Mr. Akpi's Compound

Edirin walks reluctantly into the compound. As he walks past the black 2001 Toyota Camry his father bought some months ago, towards the main door of the bungalow, he couldn't hold himself from admiring and running his hand over its entire length. He walks to the main door of the bungalow, knocks on the door and waits for a response.

Mrs. Elohor: Yes? Who is at the door?

Edirin: It's me, Edirin.

Mrs. Elohor opens the door and welcomes Edirin in.

Edirin: *Migwo*, ma.

Mrs. Elohor: *Vrendo*, Edirin. How are you?

Edirin: I am fine, ma.

Mrs. Elohor: This one you are here this early, hope all is well?

Edirin: All is well. I came to inform my father that I have gained admission to the university.

Mrs. Elohor: Wow! Congratulations! You are now a big boy *o*. Please, sit down, let me go inform your father that you are here. *(Leaves through the dining into the room)*

(A little while later, Mr. Akpi comes in through the dining)

Edirin: *(Bows reluctantly) Migwo,* sir.

Mr. Akpi: *Vrendo.* How are you? *(Sits on the sofa opposite the one Edirin is occupying)*

Edirin: I am fine, sir.

Mr. Akpi: What about your younger sister and your mother?

Edirin: They are both fine, sir.

Mr. Akpi: If you are all fine, so why are you here this early morning?

Edirin: I came to tell you that I have gained admission to the university.

Mr. Akpi: Is that why you came all the way from your mother's house this early morning?

Edirin: My mum said I should come this early so that I can meet you before you leave for work.

Mr. Akpi: Okay, I have heard you. *(Stands to leave)*

Edirin: I will need money for my school fees and accommodation.

Mr. Akpi: I don't have money *o*. I have not been paid my salary for the past two months.

Edirin: I know that is what you will say.

Mr. Akpi: *(Shocked to hear such words from Edirin)* What did you say?

Edirin: That is what you always say anytime I come to ask for money. I remember when I was in S. S. two, and needed a new uniform, you told me that you didn't have money. Also, when I wanted to register for WAEC, you said you didn't have money. When I came to ask for money to buy JAMB form, you also said you didn't have money, only for you to go and buy a car two days later.

Mr. Akpi: Oh! You have now grown into a man; you now talk back at me like someone talking to his mate. *(Sits back on the sofa)* The best you can do to make me know that you are now a grown up man is to start fending for yourself, and not by sitting here and talking back at me.

Edirin: I should start fending for myself? With what?

Mr. Akpi: Now listen and listen very well. My parents only trained me through primary six before they died. So, know it this day, that, it is with only primary six education that I have been able to achieve all that I have achieved in life. Here you are, I and your mother have trained you through secondary school, yet you are still not contented.

Edirin: Dad, because your parents only trained you through primary school, so you also wanted me to stop at primary school? *(Tears rolling down his cheeks)*

Mr. Akpi: I am not stopping you from getting any level of education you desire. All I am saying is that I don't have the money to train you beyond what I have done. I can't starve myself because you want more education. *(Stands and walks away through the dining)*

(Edirin remains seated for a moment as he tries to recover from the emotional shock arising from all his father had said; takes a deep breath, stands up and walks away through the main door)

Light fades.

SCENE THREE

Mrs. Titi's Compound

Edirin is spreading his washed clothes on the clothesline tied between a wooden pole and a pawpaw tree at the left corner of the compound. Miss Linda enters the compound and walks up to Edirin.

Edirin: Good morning, Aunty Linda.

Miss Linda: Morning, Edirin. How are you?

Edirin: I am fine.

Miss Linda: What about your mum?

Edirin: She has gone to the market. Any message for her?

Miss Linda: No. You are the one I've come to see.

Edirin: *(Surprised)* You came to see me? Hope there is no problem?

Miss Linda: No problem at all. Just get me a piece of paper and a pen.

Edirin: A piece of paper and a pen?

Miss Linda: Yes, get me a piece of paper and a pen.

Edirin: Okay. *(Turns and walks hesitantly into the house; then returns shortly after with a piece of paper and a pen which he hands over to Miss Linda)*

Miss Linda: *(Receives the piece of paper and the pen; writes 'prove that A + B = 0' on the paper and hands the piece of paper and pen back to Edirin)* Solve this before I return from school.

Edirin: *(Receives the paper and the pen; reads the equation slowly)* Prove that, 'A' plus 'B' is equal to zero.

Miss Linda: On my way back from school, I will stop over to get the solution. *(Turns and leaves)*

(Edirin stares at the equation for about a minute trying to think what topic such equation comes under and what possible method he could use in solving it. He picks up the empty bucket from which he had spread the clothes, turns and walks into the house; a moment later, he comes out with three different mathematics textbooks and a notebook; sits on the bench in the veranda and begins look for a solution to the equation)

Edirin: *(After about two hours of continuous writing and cancelling on the notebook, he murmurs aloud)* What kind of equation is this! I have tried all the laws and methods I can think of,

	none seems applicable. *(Gazes at the sky for a fleeting moment; gives himself a heavy slap on the head and mutters to himself)* Edirin, don't disappoint me. *(Closes his eyes and reflects for a moment, and like a vision, the idea of using the 'subject formula method' occurs to him. He tries it and it works. He leaps for joy and screams)* Yes! I have gotten it. I have gotten it.
	(Oke walks into the compound on a friendly visit; on sighting him, Edirin quickly covers the page in the notebook where he had solved the equation)
Oke:	Are you the only one at home?
Edirin:	(*Smiling broadly*) Yes *o*.
Oke:	This one you are this excited. What is happening?

Edirin: I just solved a very tricky equation. *(Pulls out the piece of paper containing the equation Miss Linda gave him and gives it to Oke)* See if you can solve this.

Oke: *(Takes a look at the equation)* What kind of equation is this? I wonder where you get all these brain-racking questions from.

Edirin: It's Linda that brought this one *o*.

Oke: Which Linda?

Edirin: That fair lady that teaches mathematics in your former school.

Oke: Don't tell me that you now attend her tutorials.

Edirin: Between me and her, who will attend each other's tutorials?

Oke: Ah! Don't tell me it's what I am suspecting *o*! Hope you know she is almost twice as old as you are. Don't let her smallish looks deceive you *o*!

Edirin: It's God that will deliver you from whatever corrupt thought that is running through your head.

Oke: Are you trying to say that she was just walking by, saw you and gave you an equation to prove?

Edirin: Yesterday, she came here to buy some stuff from my mum and met me teaching Tejiri maths. She felt I wasn't teaching her rightly because I was using those my shortcuts.

Oke: So what then happened?

Edirin: We started arguing over my methods. So, to prove to her that she is not as good as she thinks she is, I went and brought that maths question, the one I gave to Uncle John, which he couldn't solve, for her to solve.

Oke: Was she able to solve it?

Edirin: *Who born her*! When she couldn't solve it, she started saying the equation wasn't correct.

Oke: So what then happened?

Edirin: You trust me *na*! I solved it for her. And as I was solving, I was explaining to her as if it was Tejiri I was teaching.

Oke: *Chai!* This boy, you are wicked! Why will you embarrass someone like that?

Edirin: So, this morning, on her way to her school, she stopped over and gave me this to solve, (*Points to the piece of paper containing the equation Miss Linda gave him*) believing I won't be able to solve it, so that it will be that she couldn't solve mine and I too, couldn't solve hers.

Oke: Good! You think you are the only one who knows how to give people difficult equations to solve! At least, for once, someone has given you an equation you can't solve.

Edirin: Is it this simple maths that I can't solve.

Oke: It is very simple, yet you have brought three different textbooks to help you solve it.

Edirin: It was the circumstance surrounding its emergence that made me think it was difficult. All you need do is to make either 'A' or 'B' the subject formula of the equation and…

(They heard the sound of a motorcycle approaching)

Edirin: I guess she is the one coming. *(Hurriedly opens the notebook and tears out the page where he had solved the equation; Packs the three mathematics textbooks and the notebook and gives them to Oke)* Go inside and hide. I don't want her to see and begin to think you helped me in solving it.

(Oke rushes inside and hides by the window. Miss Linda enters the compound and walks up to Edirin at the veranda)

Miss Linda: This one you are beaming with excitement; I guess you have solved the equation.

Edirin: Yes, I have.

Miss Linda: How did you solve it?

Edirin: I made 'A' the subject formula of the equation, which gives me 'A' is equal to minus 'B' and then substitute the value of 'A' back into the original equation.

Miss Linda: *(Smiles)* You are indeed smart and intelligent. *(Brings out five hundred naira from her handbag and gives it to Edirin)* Have it and buy yourself a bottle of cold drink. *(Turns and leaves)*

(Oke rushes out and begins to hail Edirin)

Oke: The great mathematician of our time! The Archimedes himself! *(Remembers that he needs to pick up his younger siblings from school)* Jesus! My siblings would have closed from school *o*. I need to hurry and pick them up from their school.

Edirin: Ah! I also forgot that I need to pack my stuff for my journey tomorrow.

Oke: Is it tomorrow that you will be leaving for the university?

Edirin: Yes *o*!

Oke: I will see you when I return. *(Hurries to leave)* Keep my share of that money Linda gave you *o*.

(Edirin hurries into the house to pack his luggage for his trip)

Light fades.

SCENE FOUR

Mrs. Titi's Parlour

Edirin is lying restless on a mattress placed in the position normally occupied by the centre table which is now placed on the two-in-one sofa. He has not been able to sleep all through the night. After a while, he seats up and begins to think aloud.

Edirin: If I must complete this journey I'm about to begin, I have to try all I can to get one of those year-one scholarships Jite talked about. *(Pauses for a while and then smiles)* In five years' time, I will become an engineer, get employed by one of these oil companies and become rich…

(Mrs. Titi comes in from the room and is surprised to see Edirin awake)

Mrs. Titi: You are not sleeping?

Edirin: Mum, I couldn't sleep.

Mrs. Titi: Why couldn't you sleep? Is there any problem?

Edirin: No, mum. I just couldn't sleep.

Mrs. Titi: I guess it's the anxiety of the new phase of life you are about to begin.

Edirin: Yes, mum.

(Mrs. Titi lifts a stool from beside the two-in-one sofa, places it close to the mattress and sits)

Mrs. Titi My son, in a few hours, you will begin the journey of a new phase of your life. *(Pauses briefly then continues)* And your future depends on the choices you make in this phase. There will always be two options, and the one you choose determines the kind of life you will have after this phase. It will be up to you to choose whether you will give more attention to reading your books or doing something else; whether you will keep good company that will encourage you to be serious with your studies or bad gang; whether you...

(Edirin adjusts himself and leans his back onto the sofa opposite Mrs. Titi as he listens attentively, while she continues. After about thirty minutes of powerful advice from Mrs. Titi, a cock crows offstage)

Mrs. Titi: *(Looks at the clock on the wall)* Ah! It's already 4:52 a.m. The *keke* man that will take you to the park, will soon be here. I asked him to come by 5:30 a.m. Go and get ready.

Edirin: Okay, mum.

Mrs. Titi I hope you have packed everything you need?

Edirin: Yes, I have.

Mrs. Titi: Okay. Quickly, go take you bath and get ready.

Edirin: Okay, mum. *(Rises from the mattress, carries it and walks towards the room)*

Light slowly fades

Six years later…

SCENE FIVE

Mrs. Titi's Compound

Edirin is weeding grasses around the pawpaw tree at the left corner of the compound. Oke walks in on a friendly visit.

Oke: O-boy, you have added weight *o*.

Edirin: My brother, I don't know where this weight is coming from *o*! And I don't even eat that much *sef*.

(They both laugh, shake hands and hug each other)

Edirin: When did you return?

Oke: I came back last night. When did you return from Akwa Ibom?

Edirin: I returned that same POP day; in fact, I went with my luggage to the NYSC secretariat where I collected my discharge certificate. And as soon as I got it, I went straight to the park.

Oke: That means you have been back since four days ago?

Edirin: Is it up to four days now?

Oke: Don't tell me you have forgotten the day we did our POP so soon!

Edirin: *(Smiles)* See how time flies!

(Edirin leads Oke as they walk to the bench under the mango tree at the right corner of the compound and sit down)

Edirin: O-boy, what happened to you?

Oke: I don't understand what you mean.

Edirin: You look darker!

Oke: Ah! *(Smiles)* That is what I got from serving my fatherland *o*!

Edirin: How?

Oke: The sun in Maiduguri is something else. If you walk under it for just five minutes, this your skin that is looking like this, will turn black.

Edirin: Thank God, I wasn't posted to such a place.

Oke: My brother, how are your mum and Tejiri?

Edirin: They are fine *o*. Tejiri has gone back to school.

Oke: What level is she now?

Edirin: Year two.

Oke: Your mum is trying *o*!

Edirin: She is more than trying! I pray I get a job and start making money as soon as possible, so that she can start enjoying the fruit of her labour.

Oke: Me too. I need to start making money, so that I can start taking care of my parents and younger ones. I want to start a farming business.

Edirin: What do you mean by farming business?

Oke: I will get some planting seedlings and plant; when they mature, I will harvest and sell. I will also add poultry.

Edirin: *(Laughs sarcastically)* Just say you want to become a farmer. *(Touches Oke on his forehead with the back of his palm, mimicking an attempt to feel his temperature)*

Ah! You have malaria and it has affected your thinking.

Oke: I don't have any malaria and nothing has affected my thinking.

Edirin: *(Gives Oke a stern look)* After spending all these years in the university, farming is what you want to do. It's not as if you even studied agriculture in the university. I trust your father; he will disown you.

Oke: Those are the exact misconceptions that have made most university graduates jobless and poor in life.

Edirin: What misconceptions?

Oke: Just like you, they see their university education solely as a training to become employable and that they can only apply their university training in the discipline which is written on their certificates.

Edirin: I am talking about how my university education will help me get employment from companies like Agip, Shell or Total and be receiving salaries in millions, while you want to use yours to become a farmer. So who between us, is having misconceptions about university education? In fact, yours is worse than misconception, it is the highest level of insult and abuse of university education.

Oke: If you know the kind of money they make from farming business, you won't be saying this.

Edirin: Where is this coming from! You have never been to a farm before, neither is any of your relatives a farmer. So, someone has definitely been feeding you with the lie, that there is money in farming.

Oke: Nobody is feeding me with lies. I got to know this during service. I did my PPA in a multinational agricultural firm. Though it's a private firm and I don't know how the Alhaji managed to get corps members to be posted to him, but I can tell you that he makes so much money from the farming business.

Edirin: So, because an Alhaji in the North, who probably farms on a large scale is making plenty money, that's why you want to start a farming business? Do you know how he started?

Oke: Yes, I did. During my service, the Alhaji developed an instant liking towards me and made me one of his PAs. Normally, corps members are not allowed to go to the farming areas; our duties start and end within the administrative building. But the Alhaji always asked me to go with him whenever he was going for his routine inspection in the farms.

Edirin: Oh! Because the Alhaji made you his PA, that is the reason you want to become a farmer.

Oke: On many occasions, the Alhaji told me how he started very small and shared many secrets in the farming business with me. Before I left, I told him that I was considering starting the farming business when I return home to the South. He said it was a very good idea and that whenever I am ready, I should let him know; that he will send fertilizers and planting seedlings to me.

Edirin: I don't even know why I am listening to you. Right from our secondary school days, I have known that you like a life of suffering. I thought going to the university would change it, but it's obvious, suffering is in your DNA and it cannot be removed. *(Stands up to leave)* I have prepared copies of my CV. By Monday, I will go to the city and submit them to different companies. If you like, prepare yours so that we can go together, if you like don't. *(Goes and resumes his weeding of the grasses)*

Light fades.

Ten months later…

SCENE SIX

Mrs. Titi's Living Room

Edirin is lying on the two-in-one sofa in the living room, his ears plugged with a pair of earphones connected to his phone. Mrs. Titi enters from the room, ready to leave for work, and is surprised to see Edirin in such a state.

Mrs. Titi: Edirin, you are not dressed! Have you forgotten that, that our church member said you should be there before eight o'clock this morning to start work?

Edirin: *(Takes off the earphones from his ears as he sits up)* I didn't forget, mum.

Mrs. Titi: So, why are you not getting ready to go? Or do you want to be late on your first day at work?

Edirin: Mum, I am not going.

Mrs. Titi: You said what!

Edirin: I can't spend five years in the university and graduate as the best in the department of petroleum engineering only to come and work as a pump attendant with a twenty-thousand-naira salary.

Mrs. Titi: But it's for the meantime. You should manage it while waiting for a job from one of those companies you have submitted your CV to. It's better than sitting at home from morning till night doing nothing.

Edirin: Mum, I'll rather remain at home from morning till night than take a job of twenty thousand naira per month.

Mrs. Titi: I know that the salary is small, but it's better than sitting at home doing nothing.

Edirin: Not even an office kind of work, but as a pump attendant where anyone that is passing will see me (*He hisses in disgust*).

Mrs. Titi: And what is wrong if they see you?

Edirin: Mum, don't you know it's embarrassing for me, a graduate to be doing such work!

Mrs. Titi: I don't know what is embarrassing about that. Anyway, I won't force you to accept it. I just don't want you to continue staying idle, because, the idle mind is the devil's workshop. *(Picks her* *shoes which had been lying beside the sofa and puts them on)* Let me go and open my shop before my customers go to other shops. *(Carries her handbag and walks towards the door)*

Edirin: Bye, mum.

Mrs. Titi: *(Remembers an errand she needs Edirin to run for her; walks back to him, brings out some money from her handbag and gives to him)* Later in the afternoon, go and call the electrician to come and check what is wrong with our light. *(Turns and leaves)*

Edirin: Okay, mum. *(Puts on his earphones again and resumes his position on the sofa)*

Light fades.

SCENE SEVEN

Along the Street

Edirin is on his way to the electrician's shop to perform his mother's errand when he runs into Rume, whom he hadn't seen since they both left secondary school. As they shake hands and hug, he hails Rume by the nickname his classmates had given him because of his ebony-black complexion and his trousers which were usually high above his ankles.

Edirin: The *Aboki* himself! Is this you? I can't believe my eyes.

Rume: Yes *o*, it is I, the only guy who once beat you in mathematics.

(They both laugh and shake hands again)

Edirin: So you still remember that!

Rume: Will I ever forget that? Do you know the respect that alone earned me?

Edirin: *(Smiles)* You haven't changed one bit; you are still the same very funny Rume.

Rume: I wish I could say the same about you. You have so transformed. Look at you, slim Edirin of those day!

Edirin: *(Smiles)* It's really been a long time.

Rume: Yes *o*! Since we left secondary school, we haven't seen each other.

Edirin: Immediately we left secondary school, I gained admission to Uniben to study petroleum engineering. I heard you also gained admission that year.

Rume: I gained admission to Uniport, graduated and went for service almost two years ago.

Edirin: Wow! That's great. Me, I returned from service about ten months ago.

Rume: So, where do you work?

Edirin: I have not been able to get a job *o*! And it's so frustrating.

Rume: *(Smiles)* If you that finished service just ten months ago and haven't gotten a job, say it is frustrating, what will people like me, who returned from service and have been searching for a job for about two years now, say?

Edirin: It's beginning to look like our going to the university was a waste *o*.

Rume: My brother, education in this country is a scam. People have been saying it, but I refused to accept it, until I went for an interview last month. If you see the crowed of graduates struggling and fighting for a fifty-thousand-naira job. At a point, I said to myself, 'if all the money and time I spent in the university and the stress I endured is to come and fight for a fifty-thousand-naira job, whereas, those who didn't go to school can easily get a thirty- or forty-thousand-naira job, then truly, education in this country is indeed a scam.

Edirin: It's really disheartening. After spending such a huge amount of money and time, you won't get a job.

Rume: Meanwhile, if you see what some young boys whom I am very sure didn't even complete secondary school, were doing with money at the wedding of my maternal cousin which I attended last week!

Edirin: What were they doing?

Rume: They were spraying and throwing one thousand naira bills in bundles. If you see the kind of cars they drove.

Edirin: All these children of politicians! After their fathers have stolen public money, they will be spending it anyhow.

Rume: Who said they were politicians' children? They are yahoo boys!

Edirin: No wonder.

Rume: All those years I spent in the university, if I had used them in doing yahoo, by now I would have been a multi-millionaire.

Edirin: That is true *o*. Even if it was a business one had invested all those money and years in, one would have made so much profit.

Rume: No business will give you as much money as yahoo would. And that is why I have made up my mind to start it.

Edirin: You want to start yahoo? Do you know how to do it?

Rume: I have discussed with someone that has agreed to teach me. He promised to invite me to his house whenever he is ready.

Edirin: Please, let me know whenever he invites you. I will like to go with you. I want to also learn.

Rume: I don't know if he will agree. It was one of my cousins that spoke to him on my behalf.

Edirin: He will. Just talk to that your cousin, and ask him to also talk to the person on my behalf too. Tell him that I am your good friend.

Rume: Even if he agrees, the arrangement is that, I will go and live with him in the city *o*. The question is, will your parents allow you to go and live with a total stranger?

Edirin: Why not!

Rume: Okay, I will call and talk to my cousin about you when I get home, and ask him to talk to the guy. And if the guy agrees, I will call you to join me whenever I want to go and see him.

Edirin: That is my original guy! Thank you very much.

Rume: Don't thank me yet *o*. I don't know if he will agree *o*.

Edirin: I know he will. So, let me quickly go run my mum's errand, so that I won't have any engagement. Who knows, he might call you any moment from now. *(Shakes hands with Rume as a way of saying goodbye)*

Rume: O-boy! See enthusiasm!

Edirin: No time to waste *o*. Man needs to start making money as soon as possible.

Rume: Okay, I will call you.

(They both give each other a hug and continue their journeys in opposite directions)

Light fades.

Few days later…

SCENE EIGHT

Andy's Mansion

In one of the guestrooms in Andy's duplex, Edirin, Rume, Kome and Ogaga are seated randomly in the well-furnished air-conditioned room. Each has a laptop with which he is surfing the Internet as they familiarize and chat with one another.

Rume: How long have you two been here?

Ogaga: This is my third month; while Kome have been here for over seven months.

Edirin: Wow! That means you people must have been paid several times by some *magas*.

Ogaga: You think it's that easy, *abi*? It was just last week that I managed to get my first *maga* to pay seven hundred dollars, and Boss praised me for it. He said it usually takes most newbies much longer to get their first pay.

Edirin: Does that mean Kome has not been able to get any *maga* to pay him?

Ogaga: He has been paid twice. But he got his first payment after five months.

Kome: Ogaga, why do you like to always reduce my glory?

Ogaga: How? What do you mean?

Kome: Why will you say it is two times that I have been paid by my *magas*?

Ogaga: Is it not twice that your white-mama has sent you money?

Kome: What about the one that was sent by that troublesome *maga*?

Ogaga: Oh! Sorry, I forgot that one.

Edirin: (*Stands up from where he is sitting and walks to the air-conditioner switch and puts it off*) O-boy, I can't pretend and kill myself with pneumonia o. My liver and kidneys are beginning to freeze.

(*Rume and the others burst into laughter*)

Edirin: You people's laughter has made me to forget what I wanted to ask Kome. (*Pauses for a moment as he tries to recall what it is he wanted to ask Kome*) Okay, I now remember. Kome, you said 'before her job *cast*' what do you mean by that?

Kome: It means before her job get spoiled.

Edirin: And how did her job got spoiled?

Kome: The *maga* discovered that I was scamming her and refused to send any more money.

Edirin: I pray it doesn't take me long before I get a *maga* to pay me *o.*

Ogaga: Is there any one of us who didn't pray and wish that at the beginning? But wishes were not horses.

(*Andy, their master, comes in to check on them. They all greet him*)

Andy: This room is hot. Is the air conditioner bad?

Kome: It was Edirin who switched it off. He said he was catching cold.

Rume: You shouldn't blame him. He has been trekking under the sun for the past one year looking for employment, and he is now used to the hot-poverty-environment.

(*Ogaga and Kome burst into laughter*)

Edirin: You are mad! It's your father that is used to poverty-hot environment. You and I who has trekked more under the sun!

Andy: Well, I came to check and see how you two are settling in. It is obvious you guys have settled in perfectly. Ogaga, come let's go get some stuff from the supermarket. *(Turns and leaves; Ogaga rises and follows him)*

Light fades.

Five months later...

SCENE NINE

Andy's Compound

Edirin is seated absentminded on one of the chairs in the balcony. Rume comes out and sees Edirin lost in thought. He taps Edirin to bring him out of his absentmindedness and enquires what he is thinking about.

Rume: Edirin, what is the issue? You looked worried.

Edirin: Why won't I be! This is the fifth month, and I have not been able to convince any *maga* to pay me.

Rume: Neither have I. But I am not worried because I know when the time comes, *magas* will start paying me from left, right and centre.

Edirin: I need to start making and spending money like other yahoo boys.

Rume: We have been told that it takes consistent chatting with the clients and patience. Unless, you want to do *yahoo-plus*.

Edirin: What do you mean by 'unless I want to do *yahoo-plus*'? Does that mean that it helps one to get a *maga* to pay him faster?

Rume: Don't tell me that you don't know what *yahoo-plus* is!

Edirin: Please, stop asking me childish question! If I knew about it wouldn't I have been doing it?

Rume: So you mean you would have been using diabolic powers from a native doctor to hypnotize your *magas* to send you money! Because that is what *yahoo-plus* means.

Edirin: And how is that possible? One will be here and be hypnotizing someone in another faraway country.

Rume: It is very possible *o*. (*Looks left and right to be sure no one else is around to hear what he wants to say*) In fact, I know of a yahoo guy in my maternal village that is doing *yahoo-plus*. And there is a rumour that he left his laptop in the shrine of the one-eyed native doctor in the neighbouring village for seven days and ever since he took it back, all his *magas* have been paying him left, right and centre.

Edirin: So you knew all these, yet you allowed us to waste the past five months of our lives struggling to get *magas* to pay us. Is there any act that can be more wicked than that!

Rume: God forbid that insinuation of yours! I will never go to a native doctor or his shrine.

Edirin: But what is wrong in just going to drop your laptop in a native doctor's shrine and after seven days you go and take it back? Or did the rumour say he killed or used any of his family members for sacrifice?

Rume: Even if he didn't use any of his family members for sacrifice, don't you know that anything that has to do with native doctor always has negative consequences?

Edirin: Well, everybody is entitled to his or her opinion, and that is yours. *(Stands up to leave)* Before I forget, what is the name of your maternal neighbouring village where the one-eyed native doctor lives?

Rume: It is Ukpedi. It is the village before my maternal village. Don't tell me you intend going there *o*.

Edirin: If it doesn't bother you that it's been five months, yet neither of us has been able to get a *maga*, it bothers me. And if going to visit the one-eyed native doctor will make it easy for me to get one as soon as possible, then first thing tomorrow morning, I will leave for Ukpedi.

Rume: I trust Boss Andy; he will never permit you to leave this house for such journey.

Edirin: And you think I will be that daft to tell him?

Rume: Even if you are able to sneak out and make such a trip without him knowing, do you think you can be in this house without your laptop for seven whole days and he won't notice?

Edirin: (*Pauses for a moment as he tries to think of a possible way of embarking on the journey without Andy knowing*) I think I know what to do.

Rume: Whatever your plans are, count me out *o*.

Edirin: Look at you! Bad luck personified, saying I should count you out of my plans, as if I added you in my plans. Don't you know that adding you in my plans is like carrying a bucket of water and pouring it into the fire I am using to prepare food for myself?

Rume: You are mad. It is your ancestor that is bad luck personified.

(*They both laugh*)

Edirin: All I need you to do for me, is let this remain between me and you.

Rume: You can trust me on that. But I still strongly advise that you shouldn't get yourself involved in *yahoo-plus o.*

Edirin: Chief adviser, your advice is not needed. (*Picks up his phone from the chair and walks into the living room*).

Light fades.

Ten days later...

SCENE TEN

Andy's Sitting Room

Edirin, Ogaga, Rume and Andy (The Boss) are seated in the dining section of the sitting room, each browsing the Internet with the laptop in front of him.

Ogaga: Edirin, what's up with the client that you sent an account number to yesterday? She hasn't paid yet?

Edirin: The last time I spoke with her, she said she was on her way to the bank to do the cash transfer.

Andy: Wow! In no distant time, you would get your first pay. I can see you are already beaming with joy.

Edirin: (*Smiles*) The Boss, that is not what is even making me joyful. Do you remember that client that had agreed to send me ten thousand dollars and all of a sudden stopped responding to my chats and calls?

Ogaga: Is there anyone in this house that will forget the client whose disappointment almost made you run mad?

Rume: What about her?

Edirin: Look at the message she sent me few hours ago. (*Turns the screen of his laptop towards Rume and Ogaga*)

(*Rume and Ogaga scan through the message on Edirin's laptop quietly*)

Ogaga: This is a miracle!

Rume: Please, don't involve God in this.

(Edirin looks at Rume; and with eye and body movements, pleads with him not to say anything concerning his visit to the one-eyed native doctor)

Andy: Let me see the message. (*Turns the screen of Edirin's laptop from Rume and Ogaga's direction towards himself; as he is reading the message, an incoming message icon pops up on the top right corner of the screen*) You have a message from Melisa.

Edirin: The Boss, what did the message say?

Kome: (*Opens the message by clicking on the icon*) It's a payment receipt of two thousand.

Ogaga: (*Jumps out of his seat; goes to Edirin and hugs him*) Congratulations! You have finally broken the jinx for yourself and Rume.

Andy: This calls for celebration. (*Takes a look at the time on his cell phone*) 3:56 a.m. It's already too late to start going to a club. Rume, get some bottles of champagne from the fridge let's have a preamble. Later in the day, we are shutting down the club.

Edirin: By then, I believe the other client would have paid in the ten thousand.

(*Rume leaves to get the bottles of champagne for the preamble celebration as requested by Andy*)

Light fades.

SCENE ELEVEN

Andy's Sitting Room

Ogaga is holding a bottle of champagne, dancing to the song playing on the sound system, while Edirin and Andy are seated flamboyantly on adjacent sofas separated by the centre table loaded with bottles of champagne and other expensive wines, as they celebrate and discuss Edirin's plan of building a duplex for his mother.

Edirin: The Boss, when did the guy drawing the building plan say it will be ready?

Andy: He promised to bring two different designs this evening for you to make a choice.

Edirin: So, the engineer can commence building this week!

Andy: That will depend on how soon you are able to reach an agreement with the engineer.

Don't forget that you have to get the plan approved by the government.

Edirin: My mother has suffered so much, it's time for her to enjoy herself. (*Drinks from the glass of wine he is holding*) I just want to start and complete the building as soon as possible, so that I can now settle down and look for a good house uptown to buy for myself.

Andy: That is money talking. (*Hails Edirin*) The latest millionaire in town.

Edirin: My father literally abandoned us, leaving the responsibilities of both mother and father to her alone.

Andy: That is the typical behaviour of an Urhobo man. They always leave the responsibility of taking care of the children to their wives, though it's changing gradually. Some Urhobo men do take care of their children these days.

(Kome comes in with takeaway packages of rice and chicken and wraps of barbecued fish which he was sent to buy from an eatery; adjusts the bottles of wine on the table to create space, and places the takeaway packages on the table. He takes a bottle of wine, pops it open and goes to join Ogaga in dancing to the song playing from the sound system. Edirin unwraps one of the barbecued fish and pinches off a piece… His phone rings. He receives the call and presses the phone his ear)

Edirin: Yes, this is Edirin Akpi (*Listens for a moment. Signals Ogaga to turn down the volume of the sound system; takes the phone off his ear and presses the speak-out button*) I didn't hear you clearly. Can you repeat what you just said?

Caller: I said, I am calling you from NLNG, with respect to the interview you attended some months ago.

Edirin: Okay.

Caller: I am pleased to inform you that you have been offered employment. So, kindly come and collect your employment letter and resume duty immediately. Once again, congratulations.

Edirin: Okay. Thank you for your call; but I am no longer interested, I now have a better job. (*Ends the call*) Useless people! Interview that I attended over seven months ago, it's now they are calling me for employment. If I was relying and waiting for that employment, wouldn't I have died of frustration and hunger?

Ogaga: Don't mind them, useless people!

Edirin: Please, put on the music and let the fun continue. (*Takes a piece of chicken in one hand and his glass of champagne in the other, stands and begins to dance to the song playing on the sound system*)

(*Andy pinches off a piece from the barbecued fish and eats it; takes his glass of wine and joins Edirin. Kome and Ogaga each picks a piece of chicken in one hand and a glass of wine in the other hand and joins Edirin in dancing to the song playing on the sound system*)

Light fades.

SCENE TWELVE

Along Uloho Village Square Road

Edirin in his newly acquired car is on his way to the site where he is building a duplex for his mother. He sees Oke walking down the road; he winds down the glass of his car and hails him.

Edirin: Oke, the business farmer! (*Stops the car beside Oke*)

Oke: (*Surprised*) Edirin! (*Steps backwards and admires the car*) Wow! Is this your car?

Edirin: (*Smiles*) You haven't changed this your habit of asking dummy questions.

Oke: Please pardon me. (*Admires the car for the second time*) This is a machine!

Edirin: (*Smiles*)

Oke: I guess you finally got a job in one of these big oil companies.

Edirin: (*Smiles*) How is your farming business going? (*Looks at Oke from head to toe in mockery*)

Oke: We are progressing gradually. How are your mother and Tejiri?

Edirin: They are very fine. I am on my way to the site where I am building a house for her, to see how far the workers have gone.

Oke: Wow! You are building a house for your mother! She will be so happy.

Edirin: That woman has suffered for too long. It's time for her to enjoy the fruit of her labour.

Oke: I pray that one day; I too will be able to build for my parents.

Edirin: Hope you are not relying on this madness you call farming business for that prayer to come true?

(*Oke's cell phone beeps*)

Oke: Excuse me. (*Brings out the phone from his pocket; it's an alert of an email. He opens and reads the email silently for a short while and then screams with joy*)

Edirin: Why are you screaming like a mad man?

Oke: The partnership project I have been pursuing for the past one year has just been approved. (*Skims through the email again and screams more loudly*)

Edirin: Can you please stop screaming like a mad man!

Oke: I need to hurry home. I will call you later.

(*Edirin stares at Oke as he walks away hurriedly*)

Light fades.

SCENE THIRTEEN

The Palace of His Royal Majesty, the King of Uloho Kingdom

His Royal Majesty, King Koko and his favourite chief, Chief Tovie are seated in the palace discussing the success of the just concluded festival of maidens. Chief Tovie adjusts himself on his chair leaning forward towards the centre table; he takes the bottle of local gin and the low-ball glass beside it from the table, half-fills the low-ball glass with gin from the bottle and empties it into his mouth; places the low-ball glass and the bottle back on the table.

Chief Tovie: Your Majesty, the festival of maidens has never been this glorious. It is the talk of the town and even neighbouring towns. The wrestling competition and the free food for all took the festival to a new climax.

King Koko: May the gods be praised. And thanks to you who brought the idea of introducing a wrestling competition among the events of the festival.

Chief Tovie: More thanks to you, Your Majesty, because if you had not accepted the idea, nobody would have known it will add so much colour to the festival.

(One of the palace attendants comes in, walks to King Koko and whispers to him that he has some visitors. King Koko with a wave, authorizes the palace attendant to bring the visitors in. The palace attendant leaves, then returns almost immediately accompanied by Oke and his associate. Oke and his associate bow and greet King Koko, while the palace attendant bows and takes his leave.)

Oke: Your Majesty, may you live long.

(*King Koko waves his* adjudju *as a sign of acceptance of Oke's greetings*)

Oke: (*Turns to Chief Tovie*) Good afternoon, sir.

Chief Tovie: Good afternoon, gentlemen. (*Points to Oke*) Your face looks... Oh! I remember. You are the owner of the yam farm.

Oke: Yes, sir.

Chief Tovie: What is that your name again?

Oke: My name is Oke, sir. Oke Edewor.

Chief Tovie: Yes, that was what you said that day.

King Koko: It's obvious you two have met somewhere before.

Chief Tovie: Your Majesty, this is the anonymous man that gave us all the tubers of yam we used during the festival, free of charge.

King Koko: Wow! Such a young man! And by the name Oke, you must be from one of our near or distant neighbouring towns.

Oke: (*Smiles*) I am from this town, Your Majesty. I am one of your subjects, sir.

King Koko: (*Surprised*) One of my subjects! But I don't think I have seen your face before. Who is your father?

Oke: My father is Joseph Edewor, the old soldier.

King Koko: You mean Joseph, the old soldier is your father?

Oke: Yes, Your Majesty.

King Koko: No wonder! That explains why I don't know you. It's only recently that your father is beginning to associate with his kinsmen. Those early years that he returned to the community after his retirement from the Nigerian army, he refused to socialize with other of his kinsmen and was even preventing his children from mingling with other people's children.

(*Oke smiles*)

King Koko: All the same, you are indeed a son of the soil. Come close and receive your king's blessing.

(*Oke walks closer to King Koko and bows before him*)

King Koko: (*Touches Oke three times with his* adjudju) May the gods of our land bless you.

Oke: Amen, Your Majesty.

King Koko: (*Points to the vacant chairs opposite Chief Tovie*) Please, you people should sit down and tell us what brought you to the palace.

(*Oke and his associate bow and take their seats*)

Oke: Your Majesty, for the past one year, I have been pursuing a partnership project with a multinational agricultural firm where I did my primary assignment during NYSC, to establish a palm tree plantation and a palm oil factory. Having finished with the documentation aspect last week, we wish to commence the project. And I thought it will be good to site such a project in my community because it will create employment for our people and bring development to the community. So, I have come to discuss it with you, Your Majesty, and seek your approval.

Chief Tovie: Wow! This is good news. (*Takes the bottle of gin and the low-ball glass from the table; pours some gin from the bottle into the low-ball glass and gulps it down*) A palm oil factory to be situated in this community!

Oke: But that will depend on whether we are able to get the landed space needed for the project from the community.

King Koko: My son, once again, may the gods of our land bless you.

Oke: Amen, Your Majesty.

King Koko: If I may ask, what size of land are we looking at?

Oke: Your Majesty, its twelve acres that will be needed for the project.

Chief Tovie: This is a massive portion of you are talking about!

King Koko: My son, I have heard you. (*Pauses for a moment*) What you came for is a very delicate matter. Even though I am the king, I can't solely give you an approval on such delicate matters. I will have to discuss it with my council of chiefs. Therefore, I will request that you come back in two days' time.

(*Chief Tovie nods in agreement with King Koko's decision to discuss the matter with the council of chiefs before giving Oke an approval*)

Oke: (*Bows*) May you live long, Your Majesty. In that case, may we take our leave, to return in two days' time.

(*Oke and his associate stand, bow and take their leave*)

Light fades.

Five years later…

SCENE FOURTEEN

Kome's Sitting Room

Edirin, obviously still in shock from the night's incident, is seated dejectedly. Rume and Kome are seated on the three-in-one sofa opposite Edirin commiserating with him.

Rume: This is really strange! Not even a pin could be salvaged?

Edirin: I just wish this is a dream and that I will wake up to see that none of this happened!

Kome: How did it really happen?

Edirin: (*Takes a deep breath, then shakes his head*) I really don't know what happened. It was from my sleep I began hearing shouts of fire, fire, fire… At first it was as though I was dreaming. The shouts continued, gradually becoming louder and louder, and eventually woke me up to see that even my bedroom was already on fire, with smoke everywhere. I can't even tell how I got out of that room and out of the compound.

Rume: I am beginning to think that these are not ordinary.

Edirin: What is not ordinary?

Rume: Since this year, it's been one misfortune after another that has befallen each of us. First, it was Kome's wife of less than two years that died during child bearing; then Andy and Ogaga's EFCC case which has kept them in EFCC detention for two months now. And with the way the investigation is going, it might end with the government confiscating all their property. And now, this mysterious fire incident that has destroyed almost everything you had.

Kome: Rume, please don't start! I am not in the mood for those your talks of the curses from our clients being responsible for this and that *bla bla bla.* (*Stands from his seat, walks to Edirin and pats him consolingly*) Bad things happen to make a man stronger. Put your loss behind, put yourself together and move on with life. Let me go and put on my shirt so that we can go get you some clothes and a phone for a start. (*Turns and exits through one of the inner doors*)

Edirin: Don't worry, I know where to go find out if this was ordinary or not.

Rume: And where could that be?

Edirin: I will go to that one-eyed native doctor; he will be able to tell me if this fire incident was ordinary or not. I pray that I should still be able to find my way to his shrine and… (*Hears footsteps approaching and stops talking)*

Kome: (*Walks in from the same door he had exited; and picks up his car key from the centre table*) Let's go.

(*Edirin and Rume stand and join Kome, then they all exit through the front door*)

Light fades.

SCENE FIFTEEN

The Palace of His Royal Majesty, King Koko

His Royal Majesty, King Koko, and some members of his council of chiefs, are seated as they discuss and finalise arrangements for the forthcoming festival of maidens.

Chief Tovie: Your Majesty, having confirmed the dates for the festival, I think the town crier should be asked to go and announce it to the villagers.

King Koko: Oh yes, you thought well. (*Turns to the palace guard by his side*) Send two messengers to go and call the town crier right away.

(The palace guard bows and leaves)

Chief Osiobe: You Majesty, I think I can now go ahead with the production of the invitation letters?

King Koko: Yes, you can. In fact, the invitation letters have to be ready today. So that we can start distributing them. You know we don't have much time.

Chief Tovie: Chief Osiobe, your mention of invitation has reminded me! Your Majesty, you haven't said anything concerning the invitation from our illustrious son, for the commissioning of his ultra-modern palm oil factory. The event is this weekend.

King Koko: Oh, oh, oh, I totally forgot. We all have to be there. That young man is the pride of this village.

Not only has he created employment for our people, he has also placed the name of this village in a position of recognition on the map of this state and even the country.

Chief Osiobe: You are very correct, Your Majesty. The least we can do to encourage him, is to honour his invitation.

King Koko: We will do much more than that to encourage him. We will honour him during the festival and bestow on him a chieftaincy title.

Chief Osiobe: Your Majesty, your wisdom is not of this world! May you live forever.

Chief Tovie: Your Majesty, that is a wonderful idea. It will add more glamour to this year's festival. But the question is, will the young man accept a chieftaincy title?

King Koko: Why won't he accept?

Chief Tovie: On different occasions that I and others have met him to make him chairman of an event or offer him an award, he turned it down, saying, he didn't want anything that will attract public attention towards himself.

Chief Osiobe: Chief Tovie is very correct. Those were his exact words on one or two occasions that I have approached him on the same subject matter. But since this is coming from Your Majesty, I doubt if he will turn it down.

King Koko: In that case, I will personally talk to him about it.

Chief Tovie: Maybe if Your Majesty talks to him personally, he will accept. (*Looks at his wrist watch*) Ah! it's already past 5 p.m. Your Majesty, I need to rush home. My daughter says a young man is coming to ask for her hand in marriage this evening.

King Koko: Wow! That is good news. You better hurry home now before the young man changes his mind. *Osharegaran!*

(*They all burst into laughter*)

Chief Tovie: (*Stands up and bows to King Koko*) May you live long, Your Majesty. (*Begins to leave*)

Chief Osiobe: Please, let me join you. You will drop me off by the business centre where I will print the invitation letters. (*Stands up, bows to King Koko and joins Chief Tovie and they both leave*)

Light fades.

SCENE SIXTEEN

Igbogbo's Shrine

Igbogbo, the one-eyed juju priest, is seated on the tortoise shell which he uses as stool, pouring libations and chanting incantations to the idol in front of him. Edirin walks in, takes off his shoes as he greets Igbogbo.

Edirin: Greetings, Wise-one.

Igbogbo: *(With a wave of the hand, gives signal asking Edirin to sit down, as he continues his libations and incantations. Shortly after, takes a bottle from the short stool in front of the idol, pours some of its content into a short glass and pours it into his mouth; spews it over the idol and then turns towards Edirin, and by the help of his spiritual powers, sees something wrong about Edirin; turns towards the idol and chants* *some incantations and then turns back towards Edirin*) Ashira, the goddess of wealth and power, is not happy with you. In fact, her mark of destruction is already on you.

Edirin: (*Throws himself on the floor in front of Igbogbo*) Wise-one, have mercy. Please, have mercy.

Igbogbo: (*Turns towards the idol and chants some incantations; turns towards Edirin*) You came to the supreme goddess of wealth and power for help, and after she obliged you, you abandoned her.

Edirin: Please, have mercy.

Igbogbo: (*Turns towards the idol*) He said you should have mercy. (*Takes a bottle of local gin from beside him, chants some incantations and* *sprinkles the content of the bottle over the idols; takes a native chalk from the short stool in front of the idol, crushes it into powder in his left palm. He moves his left palm containing the crushed chalk over Edirin three times, goes to the entrance of the shrine and blows it into the air. Chants incantations as he returns and sits*) Sit down my son.

(*Edirin rises from the floor and seats on the bamboo bench*)

Igbogbo: (*Smiles*) Ashira, the merciful goddess, has decided to give you a second chance.

Edirin: (*Bows*) Thank you, Wise-one.

Igbogbo: But you must first offer a sacrifice to her. (*Turns towards the idol, chants some incantations* *and turns towards Edirin*) A human sacrifice.

Edirin: Human sacrifice!

Igbogbo: Yes, a human sacrifice. (*Picks up his wand from the short stool in front of the idol, touched the idol with the wand three times, chants some incantations and turns swiftly towards Edirin*) You will give your mother's life in place of yours.

Edirin: What? I should kill my mother?

Igbogbo: You don't have to kill her. Just bring an item of clothing that she has worn within the past one week and leave the rest to me.

Edirin: Wise-one, there should be an alternative. I can't sacrifice my mother.

Igbogbo: (*Turns towards the idol and chants some incantations*) You have seven days to offer the sacrifice or else you will run mad. (*Continues chanting incantations*)

Edirin: Wise-one, please, there should be an alternative. I can't kill my mother.

Igbogbo: Seven days or else you will run mad. Leave now before you incur the wrath of Ashira!

(*Edirin stands and hurries out; while Igbogbo continues chanting incantations*)

Light fades.

SCENE SEVENTEEN

Uloho Village Square

The entire Uloho village is filled with an aura of festivity. Light comes on stage at the beautifully decorated village square. King Koko, members of the council of chiefs and the entire villagers are enjoying themselves by the colourful display of the sheshegbe *masquerade. The villagers give loud cheers as the masquerade ends its exhilarating performance and exits the stage. The drummers change the rhythm of their beat to announce and usher in the maidens being initiated into womanhood. The crowd give a deafening joyful shout as the maidens dance in bare-bodied except for a piece of white wrapper tied around their waists with colourful beads on their necks and waists. The maidens dance rhythmically to the tunes of the drums for a while and then dance out of the stage to the bamboo bench prepared for them. Chief Tovie raises his* adjudju *as a signal to the audience to be quiet as King Koko rises up to speak.*

King Koko: Great people of Uloho kingdom, I sincerely thank all of you for your active participation in the various activities that took place these past six days of the festival of maidens. The maiden goddess of fruitfulness and fertility will bless all of you.

Villagers: *(Give a deafening shout of "amen" accompanied by drumbeats)*

King Koko: In this euphoria of joy and celebrations, I want to honour an illustrious son of this kingdom. He is the provider of employment and source of livelihood to many of our people, and has placed the name of this village in a position of recognition on the map of this state and even the country. He is none other than Oke Edewor.

Villagers: (*Applause and shouts accompanied with drumbeats*)

Oke: (*Rises deferentially from his seat, bows towards King Koko, waves to the villagers and then sits back on his seat*)

King Koko: Come to me, my son.

Oke: (*Goes towards King Koko and kneels before him*)

(*Chief Tovie brings out a collection of chieftaincy beads and an* adjudju *from the bag beside him and takes them to King Koko. King Koko* takes *the beads from Chief Tovie and wears them around Oke's neck and left wrist; then takes the* adjudju *and places it into Oke's right hand*)

Villagers: (*Applause and shouts*)

King Koko: By the power bestowed upon me by the ancestors and great people of this kingdom, I confer on you the chieftaincy of this great kingdom.

Villagers: (*Give ecstatic shouts accompanied by applause and drumbeats*)

Light fades.

SCENE EIGHTEEN

On the Premises of the General Hospital

Oke is returning from an inspection tour on his palm tree plantation. As he drives past the general hospital, he sees Tejiri walking out of the hospital looking worried. He pulls over, alights from his car and goes to her to enquire what the issue is.

Oke: Good afternoon, Barrister Tejiri.

Tejiri: (*Surprised to see Oke whom she hasn't seen for years*) Ah! Who am I seeing? I can't believe my eye. Oke! Oh please forgive me, Chief Oke. My mum told me that the King honoured you with a chieftaincy title.

Oke: (*Smiles*) How is school, and when did you return?

Tejiri: I completed my one-year law school training and came back last week.

Oke: Wow! So I wasn't wrong when I called you barrister!

Tejiri: (*smiles*)

Oke: What are you doing around the hospital premises?

Tejiri: My mum collapsed this morning. I had to rush her here. Though she has been revived, the doctor asked me to buy some more drugs. And that is what I am going for.

Oke: Was she sick?

Tejiri: No, she wasn't *o*!

Oke: What about Edirin, is he not in town?

Tejiri: (*Tears begin to roll down her cheeks*) You mean you are not aware of the fire incident that completely destroyed his house and cars in the city few weeks ago?

Oke: Jesus! So Edirin is the victim of that fire incident some of my staff were gossiping about! Where is he now and how is he doing?

Tejiri: My brother has gone mad.

Oke: What!

Tejiri: I believe he got involved with bad friends who introduced him to occultism, and now, they are requesting him to sacrifice our mother.

Oke: Blood of Jesus! (*Becomes momentarily speechless*) But how did you come about these revelations?

Tejiri: I and my mum were in the kitchen this morning preparing breakfast, when we heard him scream from the sitting room "no, I can't kill my mother". We rushed out to find out what was happening, only to find him taking off his clothes and behaving strangely. My mum couldn't take the shock of seeing her only son running mad; she collapsed immediately.

Oke: Oh my God, see what impatience has caused Edirin! (*Pauses for a moment as he tries to think out how he can help*) Come into my car let's go buy the drugs the doctor requested for you mum, then we will go and see my pastor if he can help Edirin.

(*Oke and Tejiri walk into Oke's car and he drives away*)

Light fades.

THE END...

www.ingramcontent.com/pod-product-compliance
Lightning Source LLC
LaVergne TN
LVHW041110150826
845673LV00007B/1994

* 9 7 8 9 7 8 9 9 7 0 8 1 0 *